Something is Growing

AMAZON MOVERS

Something is Growing

WALTER LYON KRUDOP

Atheneum Books for Young Readers

Atheneum Books for Young Readers
An imprint of Simon & Schuster Children's Publishing Division
1230 Avenue of the Americas
New York, NY 10020

First edition
Printed in the United States of America
10 9 8 7 6 5 4 3 2 1
The text is set in 15-point Galliard.
The illustrations are rendered in acrylic paints.
Designed by Kimberly M. Adlerman

Library of Congress Cataloging-in-Publication Data

Krudop, Walter.
Something is growing / by Walter Lyon Krudop. —1st ed.
p. cm.
Summary: When Peter plants a seed near a city street,
things very quickly get out of control.
ISBN 0-689-31940-1
[1. Plants—Fiction. 2. Gardening—Fiction.] I. Title.
PZ7.K938So 1995
[E]—dc20 94-12794

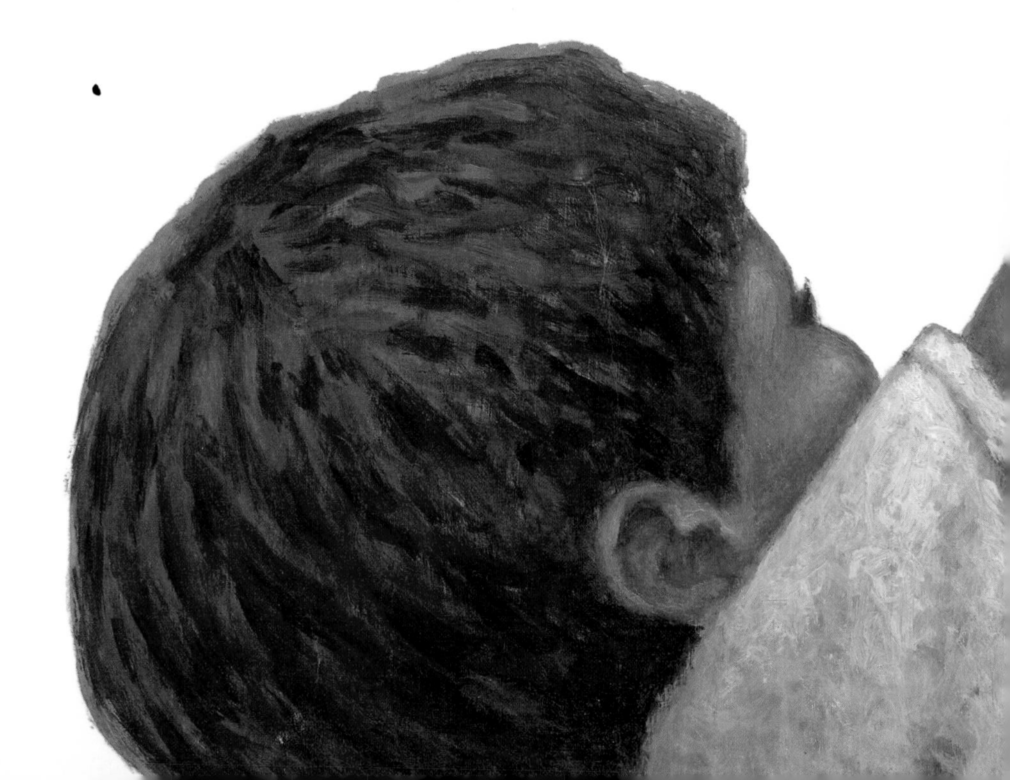

FOR THOSE OF THE FOREST,
AND THOSE OF THE CITY
—W. L. K.

Early one morning a boy named Peter planted a seed in a small patch of dirt by a city street. He watered it carefully and talked to it every day. “You’re going to grow,” Peter whispered. Nobody noticed him.

Even the neighborhood snoop, Mrs. Cadoogan, didn't notice Peter. But she noticed his plant. "I don't like this one bit. I'm going to call my friend Professor Thornbine. He should be told that something is growing."

“Impossible,” Professor Thornbine said. “Gigantus floriticus, a most unusual plant and a perfect specimen. They don’t grow by themselves, not at this latitude. Go easy there, Mrs. Cadoogan, and whatever you do . . .”

But it was too late. Before he could say *don't touch it,* Mrs. Cadoogan poked the plant with her umbrella. Like fireworks the plant burst, blowing fine dust everywhere.

"What's happening?" Mrs. Cadoogan asked.

“Precisely what I expected—the plant spores are sprouting,” the professor declared.

Peter filled his watering can.

“Can this be stopped?” Mrs. Cadoogan asked the professor.

“Keep your wits about you,” he said. “We’re going to get to the bottom of this.”

"Such complex root systems. Fascinating. Not since Madagascar have I seen anything like it."

"It's an eyesore," said Mrs. Cadoogan as she followed the professor.

Peter cut back some mushrooms so he could pack the roots with more soil.

Underpass to
Uptown trains

"And what do you propose to do about this?" Mrs. Cadoogan huffed. "We can't have trees hold up traffic."

"Fig trees—Urostigma to be exact," the professor said. "The plant growth appears to be accelerating; we must find out who or what is behind this."

Peter tended to a fern that Mrs. Cadoogan had swatted with her umbrella as she passed.

"Steady those ropes," the professor called as they hoisted him up to the forest canopy. "Have a sharp eye, Mrs. Cadoogan. I've a hunch what we're looking for is right under our noses."

Peter pruned back some branches, talking to his plants all the while.

"Keep rowing, Mrs. Cadoogan," the professor commanded. "I see something ahead."

"We're too late," the professor sighed. "But, by George, I know now what we're looking for."

"Will it ever stop growing?" Mrs. Cadoogan asked.

"It's not ours to stop," the professor answered.

"Well, I will say this, the water looks cleaner," she said as they floated down the river.

ALBERT

Mrs. Cadoogan sat down in an exhausted heap. Professor Thornbine lifted his telescope and peered into the jungle. "Now, where might . . . aha!" the professor exclaimed as he marched through the foliage.

Panting, Mrs. Cadoogan followed just in time to see the professor scale a small wall. A crowd had gathered outside the library. "At last we meet," the professor said. He bent down to shake Peter's hand. "Young lad, the city has come to admire your fine work." The crowd cheered.

"Hear! Hear!" Mrs. Cadoogan shouted, forgetting her good manners. "To think, Gigantus floriticus here in the city." Peter smiled proudly, and camera bulbs flashed to record the event . . .

. . . for the world to see.